Tales from Beyond

Edited by Paul Collins and Meredith Costain

sundance

Read all of the

 **Thrillogy** Titles

Fantasy/Horror

Dragon Tales

Ghosts and Ghoulies

Heroic Feats

Last Gasps

Tales from Beyond

Terrors of Nature

Science Fiction

Alien Invasions

Gadgets and Gizmos

It Came from the Lab . . .

Lost in Space

Techno Terror

Time Zones

Published by Sundance Publishing
P.O. Box 1326, 234 Taylor Street, Littleton, MA 01460

Copyright in individual stories remains with the authors.

First published 1999 as Spinouts by
Addison Wesley Longman Australia Pty Limited
95 Coventry Street, South Melbourne 3205 Australia
Exclusive United States Distribution: Sundance Publishing

ISBN 0-7608-4835-1

Printed in Canada

Contents

4

Ali Baba
and the
Forty Aliens

The author
Janeen Webb
talks about the story

"The original Ali Baba was a clever boy who found a robbers' cave in old Arabia. I wrote this story to see what would happen if a modern boy found a cave full of stolen treasure — especially if the thieves who hid it there turned out to be weirder than anyone imagined."

Ali Baba and the Forty Aliens

Alberto Barbarino blamed his parents for his name. They should have known that naming him after his uncle Al would cause confusion. His uncle was big Al, so Alberto was little Al, or Ali for short. With Barbarino's being the best restaurant in the neighborhood, it didn't take long for the kids in his class to start calling him Ali Baba, after that stupid story the teacher read to them.

The nickname stuck. And here he was, twelve years old and nearly an adult, still called Ali Baba, still refusing to waste his time with the kids who called him that. He didn't need them, with their skateboards and their trendy bikes and their private jokes. He had better things to do.

Ali was pretty much a loner. He read tons of comic books and talked his mother into buying him a supply of gothic black T-shirts and black jeans. He had a black denim jacket, too, though he was saving up to replace it with a leather one — black, of course. An oversized pair of black boots and a

dangling silver earring completed his outfit. With his glossy black hair spiked up with gel and his wraparound, black sunglasses making his pale skin look even paler against the black clothes, he looked pretty cool.

His older brother, Dean, said he looked creepy. Ali didn't care. He stayed away from the noise and bustle of the family restaurant, where everyone was hard at work and forever giving him errands to run. He headed for the hills, pedaling his battered bike to the outskirts of town, where the gold mines used to be.

He loved the silence of the old diggings, with their abandoned mines and weirdly shaped, rusting machinery. He spent most of his free time out there, poking around the ruins or panning for gold in the creek. And he did find valuables from time to time — little nuggets or flecks of gold, which he sold to the tourist shop when he had enough to make it worthwhile. He even went out there at night, hoping to see ghosts. But he never saw one, not even when he found the mounds that marked graves of long-forgotten people. Maybe they were too tired, after all that digging, to bother haunting their graves.

Ali thought he knew all of the old mine sites. But this

Saturday morning, he stumbled across a mine he could have sworn hadn't been there the week before.

There was something strange about the entrance to this particular abandoned gold mine. Sure, it looked like it had been dug out the hard way, by pick and shovel. And it had the usual rough-hewn wooden framework, the usual rusty piece of corrugated iron across the entrance, the usual KEEP OUT sign slapped on it in drippy paint. But something looked wrong. It was too neat.

There were crumpled cola cans and paper wrappers lying around, typical garbage you'd expect someone careless to leave after a picnic. But the grass was trampled flatter than a couple of picnickers with a blanket could have left it. And the woods around it were too quiet, as if the birds and animals were giving it a wide berth. And it smelled wrong — the dusty woods smell was overlaid with some chemical odor that Ali couldn't put a name to.

He decided to investigate. He had his flashlight. He told himself he'd just take a look. He wouldn't go too far in. He bent to pull aside the old iron cover across the entrance. It wouldn't budge. It looked flimsy, like all of the others, but Ali couldn't make it move at all. He climbed up onto the earth mound above the entrance tunnel and tried to loosen the iron from the top. Nothing happened. He gave it a good, hard kick, which hurt his foot, but the cover didn't even vibrate.

Ali's frustration was growing. He climbed back down and tried attacking the old iron with a heavy piece of timber from a scrap heap. Nothing, not even a dent. When he hit it, the tin even sounded wrong, kind of muffled. The entrance was sealed. And Ali couldn't tell what was sealing it.

Then, it happened. One minute he was alone in the little clearing, the next minute, there was the sound of feet. A lot of feet. Ali was terrified. He felt the blood drain from his pale face and his heart thump loudly in his chest. He barely had time to scramble up the nearest tree before the first of the intruders came into view. Ali counted forty of them, and they were all carrying packs and bundles of various shapes and sizes.

Ali knew they were aliens. They couldn't be anything else. They weren't bug-eyed monsters or robots or anything: they looked right, but they felt wrong. Like those models you build from pictures and diagrams that never quite come out looking like the real thing. These guys looked like humans, but they didn't act like humans. They weren't talking or looking around, just heading straight for the mine. They carried their heavy packs without effort, without even breaking a sweat. Maybe they couldn't sweat.

The chemical smell was getting a lot stronger, and Ali hoped he wouldn't choke or cry, or faint from the effort of staying still in his tree. He didn't think forty aliens would be very gentle if they caught him spying.

The aliens walked right up to the old mine entrance. The leader faced the barrier that had been giving Ali so much trouble and softly whispered, "Keep in."

That old corrugated iron didn't make a sound — it just disappeared. Now you see it, now you don't.

Ali watched open-mouthed as the aliens walked *through* it and into the mine tunnel beyond.

The entrance stayed open a few minutes, shimmering a little. There was a faint whiff of ozone in the air.

Then the door reappeared, solid as ever.

Ali waited in his tree, too scared to come down. Just as he was thinking he'd have to make a run for it, the door dematerialized again. He saw the strangers walk out into the clearing. Their bundles were gone. When the last member of the group appeared, the leader turned and murmured, "Keep out." And the barrier was back. The aliens left, as strangely as they had come, vanishing into the woods.

Ali was shaking as he climbed down, but fascinated, too. He wondered if the password would work for him. There was only one way to find out. Facing the entrance, he said, "Keep in."

The ozone smell came back, and the doorway opened. Ali was inside before he could think about it. He'd expected it to be dark, but he found himself in a softly lit chamber.

The walls were lined with shelves of experimental looking tubes and specimen jars and equipment. Maybe the aliens were collecting samples? He hoped they didn't need any live ones. A familiar gleam attracted his gaze, and Ali found himself looking at a basket full of very small gold nuggets. There was another basket of crystals of various types and even more baskets of minerals he couldn't identify.

Ordinarily, Ali wouldn't take what wasn't his, but he figured this stuff didn't belong to the aliens, either. And no one would believe his story if he told them — which he wouldn't. The aliens would never miss a few bits and pieces out of this huge hoard.

So Ali decided to help himself. He was not greedy: he quickly filled his pockets with the smaller

nuggets and hurried back outside. Turning to the entrance, he breathed the words "Keep out," watching with relief as the doorway resumed its abandoned-gold-mine disguise.

Back at his family's restaurant, Ali sidled into the kitchen and borrowed a scale to weigh his treasure. Then he hid the gold at the back of his underwear drawer and quickly returned the scale. He planned to sell the gold a little at a time, until he had enough to buy his leather jacket without attracting suspicion.

But the scale's weighing pan had been sticky, and a couple of flecks of gold stuck to the bottom. And the person who noticed was Dean, who was helping out in the kitchen because Saturday night was so busy.

And that's when the trouble started. Dean sauntered into Ali's room and said, "So how come you have so much gold that you have to weigh it? Who'd you steal it from?"

His voice was low and nasty. Ali felt his face growing hot. He tried to sound casual. "You spied on me. I found it around the old mines, if you must know."

Dean grabbed Ali and pushed him against the wall. His breath was hot and sour in Ali's face.

"Listen, creep," he said. "I know you're up to something, and if you don't let me in on it, I'll tell Dad that he should take a look in your underwear drawer. Understand?"

Ali admitted defeat. He didn't expect Dean to believe him about the aliens, but the gold was a powerful incentive. Dean was already dreaming about cars and clothes and how impressed all of the girls would be.

The next morning, a reluctant Ali rode with Dean out to the aliens' gold mine. It looked just the same as it had yesterday, and a lingering chemical odor told Ali that the aliens had been back. He wondered if they'd noticed anything.

Facing the door, he muttered, "Keep in," half hoping it wouldn't open. But it did, and Dean was through the entrance like a shot. He made a lot of noise. Dean was greedy — he'd brought a couple of backpacks to fill with whatever looked valuable.

Ali tried one more time to warn Dean not to stay too long and not to take too much. Dean glared at him. "If you're so scared you can run on home."

So Ali left, feeling miserable and betrayed.

And that was the last time he ever saw his brother.

When Dean didn't come home that night, Ali told his parents the truth. Then he told it again to the police and again to the search and rescue team. They didn't believe the stuff about aliens and magic doors, and Ali didn't push it. But the rest was believable. The small amount of gold that Ali showed them could easily have come from an abandoned mine. And the police thought Ali might have stumbled across the spot where one of the old men who still worked the diggings was storing his findings. They expected some old guy to turn up and claim he'd been robbed.

Volunteers combed the woods for days, looking for Dean. His bike was where he'd left it, untouched. Ali imagined they'd find his brother in one of those specimen jars, or worse.

But they never found him, or the exact same mine entrance that Ali described. The trouble was, it *had* looked just like all of the others, and everyone thought that Ali was too upset to remember exactly where it was.

There was a lot of fuss on TV for a few days. All kinds of experts said how dangerous the old diggings were, full of hidden mine shafts that a kid could fall down and never be found. Ali's upset family and local volunteers kept searching long after the experts went home. In the end, the authorities just labeled Dean's disappearance "accidental" and left it at that.

But the kids at school wouldn't drop it. Alberto Barbarino was a star, with press clippings and everything. He got to keep the gold. No one else claimed it, so it was finder's keepers.

And he bought his leather jacket.

But he doesn't wear it much.

Sanctuary

The author

Chris McTrustry

talks about the story

"I wondered what it would be like to take the place of someone else—to live his or her life, if only for a short time. Or perhaps for even longer. And then, if you did give up your identity, who would you become? The result was *Sanctuary*."

Sanctuary

Somehow, early in the evening, Dad missed a turn, and we got stuck on a narrow, bumpy, side road that didn't seem to lead anywhere or have any major exits.

"This obviously *isn't* the highway, David," Mom muttered. "Turn around before you get us lost."

Outside it had become *really* dark. Only half an hour ago, I'd been able to see for miles across quiet fields and plains. Occasionally, the lights of a small town or farm would glitter in the distance. Now there was nothing. And we hadn't passed another car for ages. The interior light flickered on over Mom's head, and the glove compartment clunked open.

"At least stop and check the map," Mom said.

"Why?" Dad said. "We're heading in the right direction."

"How can you tell?" Mom unfolded the map. She sighed. "I don't know where we are."

24

Leaning forward, I peered at the map over Mom's shoulder. We were *supposed* to be on the highway. But looking at the map, the highway was the region's only road — which meant we were on a road that didn't exist. Excellent!

"This is just like some of the science fiction stories I've read," I said.

"How's that, Tania?" Dad winked at me in the rearview mirror.

"Well, it's a classic scenario. The happy little family is going on their happy little vacation." Boring, was a more accurate description, but I didn't want to rock the boat. "Everything is groovy, until they lose their way and end up in some weird little town."

"Why is the town weird?" my little sister, Becky, asked. She looked at me with wide, scared eyes. Good.

"Oh, it could be a number of reasons," I said. "All of the people might be vampires. Or werewolves." I turned to Becky and bared my teeth and rolled my eyes like a lunatic. "Or they might be normal people like you and me, who like *eating* normal people like you and me!"

Becky squealed. "Stop it, Tania!"

"Yes, stop it, Tania," Mom said.

"They might even be aliens who read your mind and hypnotize you," I said quickly. "They capture you and take your place in the world. Then they conquer Earth."

"There's no such thing as aliens," Becky said.

"Of course not," Mom added. Then she screamed.

Our car was suddenly bathed in white-hot light. It was like the floodlights from the sports stadium were perched on the car's roof and turned all the way up to *maximum*.

"What the — ?" Dad swerved to the road's edge, but the light followed us.

"What's going on, David?" Mom screamed.

"I don't know!" Dad screamed back.

I knew. Aliens, no doubt about it! Then, as suddenly as the light had appeared, it disappeared. Dad stopped the car and cautiously rolled down his window.

"Probably a helicopter for herding cattle," he said, poking his head out. "Must come from a nearby ranch. I guess they don't get many visitors out this way."

"And we know why . . ." I said in my best creepy voice.

"Shut up, Tania!" Becky said.

"Yes," Mom said. "Stop all that nonsense."

"Just a helicopter." Dad eased the car back onto the road. We had barely gone a hundred yards when the car's headlights shined on a battered tin sign, on an old wooden fence. It told travelers they were entering a town called Sanctuary.

"It's not on the map," Mom muttered.

"They don't put *every* town on maps that size. Now if we had a *local* map . . ." Dad said. "Uh, oh. That's funny, we're low on gas. Very low."

"I need to go to the bathroom," said Becky.

"Sounds like it's time for a rest stop," said Dad.

"I don't think we should stop in a town called Sanctuary," I said. "It goes against all of the rules of science fiction."

"And not stopping goes against all of the rules of common sense," Dad said. "And I'd rather not be on the road right now."

"Me, too," said Becky.

The town suddenly jumped out of nowhere. The main street was brightly lit and pretty as a postcard. Dad eased the car into a gas station.

"All right, kids," Mom said. "No wandering off — "

A slamming door cut short Mom's sentence. Becky was out of the car and bolting for the restroom. Mom flung her door open and hurried after her. "Becky! Wait."

Dad grabbed his wallet and trotted over to the gas station office.

I stayed put. Okay, maybe I'd been fooling around earlier. But check out the evidence. A road that doesn't exist. Lights in the sky. And now a town that isn't on the map! Was I the only logical person in my family? It all spelled one thing — alien invasion, or cannibals, werewolves, or vampires. All right, *whatever* was happening in this town wasn't good for your health. I rolled down my window and gazed out on the main street of Sanctuary. It certainly was a quiet town. And clean. And empty. Where were all of the people?

"Hey there." I spun around to find a kid about my age leaning on the car. He was wearing baggy jeans and a sweatshirt with a cool skeleton riding a skateboard on it. "I'm Cooldude," he said. The name *really* suited him. "What's up?"

"Nothing much. We're just passing through."

"So you didn't come here for a vacation? *Everybody* comes here." Cooldude smiled. "You want to listen to some music or go skateboarding? We've got the best ramp."

"I dig skateboards, but isn't it kind of late?"

"Sanctuary is a safe town. Everyone is safe." Cooldude grinned.

I grinned back. Yeah. Now that I thought about it, Sanctuary did seem to be a very safe town.

"You can borrow my portable CD player if you want." Cooldude pushed this excellent CD player into my hands.

"I don't know if I should accept this —" I checked out the disk inside. No way! "This is my all-time favorite band!" I looked up, but Cooldude was gone.

A door opened. "Where did you get that?" It was Mom.

"I, um, borrowed it."

"From who?"

". . . um . . ."

Dad opened his door and flopped into his seat. "We're going to have to stay here tonight," he said. "The gas station is closed, and the owner is away until tomorrow."

That night I dreamed I was in bed, here in Sanctuary.

And a crowd of people had gathered around me. Except they didn't look like people. They were short with long, pointy heads. They had large, round eyes that looked like red saucers. And their skin was green! Yeah, *green*. And they didn't actually speak. They sounded like whales talking to each other. All squeaks and squeals. Aliens, right? Well, it figured. All that talk of aliens in the car got my imagination worked up. But the dream seemed so real. One time, I lifted my head up when I felt my arms being tugged and Cooldude popped up in front of me as big as life.

"Cool it," he said. "You're just dreaming."

The next morning, after breakfast, I went exploring. I walked along the main street, saying "Good morning" to all of the bright and happy people of Sanctuary. I felt like a dork after freaking out last night. Cooldude caught up with me, and we drifted over to the skateboard ramp.

We stayed at the ramp for hours — trying different tricks, goofing around, and just hanging out.

"Don't you love it here?" Cooldude said.

"Yeah," I said. "I could stay here forever." And I meant it.

Cooldude flipped his board onto the nearby sidewalk. "Catch you later," he said, as he prepared to push off.

"What about the ramp?" I said.

Cooldude shrugged. "I have to be somewhere."

That was cool. I went back to boarding. I'd just ripped down from the top of the ramp when I heard a car start up. I turned and saw that it was our car. Dad was pulling his seat belt over his shoulder and clicking it into place. Then Becky popped up between Mom and Dad, blowing a huge bubble-gum bubble. Little jerk. The car rolled toward me, and I saw someone else in the car.

Cooldude!

He looked at me as the car drew closer, and waved. Then he pushed at the skin hanging loose around his eyes. A bright green glow seeped from under the loose patches, and his huge saucer eyes glowed red. But by the time the car passed me, the skin was tight and in place. Except it wasn't Cooldude's face anymore. It was mine!

"That's so cool, dude," said a kid skateboarding past. He nodded at my sweatshirt. *Dude? Me?* I looked down and gasped. The cool skateboard-riding skeleton sat proudly on my sweatshirt.

I smiled. "Thanks."

I spun away from our car and jumped back onto my board. I'd never ridden so well before. I was in Sanctuary to stay.

Well, until the next family arrived, that is . . .

The Doll

The author
Rowena Cory Lindquist
talks about the story

"Years ago, I lived in an apartment above a very strange, old woman. She wasn't really a witch, but she looked like one. I've always been fascinated by Russian dolls, and, like everyone else, I was picked on at school. Somehow these three elements combined to help me write *The Doll*."

The Doll

My heart sank. Grunge was waiting for me.

I don't know why he picked on me. He was as big as a grownup — big and mean, with black hair cut short enough to bristle across his head.

Grunge stepped toward me, an ugly sneer on his face. "Let's see what's in the bag."

"N . . . nothing."

He lunged. I stepped away, but he was too quick, too strong. His hands closed on the shopping bag. I let go. He staggered back, tripped, and fell on his backside. The bag of flour burst, covering him in fine, white powder.

Just then, I heard the *beep beep* of a delivery truck as it backed up behind me. Grabbing what was left of the bag, I turned and darted behind the truck.

"That's right. Run!" Grunge yelled. "But I'll find out where you live!"

Shaking with relief, I hurried back to my apartment building. If only the Russian lady in my building

hadn't asked me to do her shopping. Then Grunge wouldn't have caught me.

At the door to Apartment 2, I hugged the torn shopping bag and knocked. According to Mom, our neighbor was a Russian refugee. Her name began with a "T," but the rest was unpronounceable. I knew because her mail had come to us once by mistake. When I returned the letter, she'd asked me to get her groceries.

Mrs. T. opened the door. I shoved the bag into her arms.

"It's all there, except for the flour. I had some trouble."

"Trouble, girlie?" She pronounced it "gorlie."

I tried to leave, but she caught my arm, peering into my face. "You wait here," she told me.

I didn't want to wait. She was the scariest old woman I'd ever seen. Her gray hair stood straight out like a witch's, and she even had a moustache!

Before I could slip into my apartment, she was back. Her old bathrobe flapped open to reveal skinny ankles disappearing into oversized slippers.

"Here, girlie. Matrioshka look after you." She shoved a brown paper bag into my hands.

I took it. What else could I do? It was her way of thanking me for doing her shopping.

"Uh, thanks. I'm sorry about the flour. I'd better go."

I let myself into the apartment and dropped my schoolbag. I nearly dumped the old woman's gift in the trash, but curiosity made me open it.

Inside the bag was a little wooden doll, with a painted face and clothes. It rattled when I shook it. Talk about dumb. Rattles were for babies.

Still, it was cute. I sat it on the kitchen table while I did my homework.

Mom brought home pizza for dinner. "What's this?" she asked, pushing the doll to one side.

"Uh, you know that lady, Mrs. T. — whatever?"

Mom nodded.

"I did her grocery shopping, and she gave me the doll."

Mom picked it up.

"Dumb doll," I said. "It's a rattle."

Mom laughed and snapped the doll in half.

"Hey, don't break it!"

"Look." She pulled the two halves apart to reveal another smaller doll. "And again!"

There was an even smaller doll inside.

"Cool. Give it to me." I took the third doll. It popped apart to reveal a fourth doll. "How many are there?"

Mom shrugged. "I don't know. I saw one on TV once."

I pulled the fourth doll apart and inside was yet another tiny doll. She was solid wood with the same smiling face, pink cheeks, and blonde hair tucked under her scarf.

Mom lined up the five dolls on the kitchen table from biggest to smallest. She frowned. "These don't look like cheap toys. Look at the painted detail in the dresses."

Now that I really looked, I could see how special the dolls were. I popped the little one inside the next one and so on until they all fitted inside each other. Then I shook the outside doll to hear them rattle.

"Don't do that!" Mom snapped. "I think you should give this back."

"Aw Mom — "

"Terri?" She frowned. "This looks like a real antique."

"But Mrs. T. gave it to me."

"Even if she did, it wouldn't be right to accept something so valuable."

I sighed.

Mom frowned at me. "You give it back first thing tomorrow morning before you go to school. Okay?"

I nodded.

The doll felt heavy in my hand as I knocked on Mrs. T.'s door. Some weird music was playing. I knocked again.

When she opened the door, the music hit me full force. It sounded like gypsy music, full of life and passion, and dancing violins.

I pushed the doll into her hands. "Mom says I have to give it back. It's too valuable!"

She took the doll automatically. Her old eyes looked hurt. "You not like her?"

"Mom says I can't keep it."

"There you are!" someone yelled.

I spun around. Grunge!

"I said I'd find you. Now you're gonna pay for that stunt with the flour!"

I backed into the entrance of Mrs. T.'s apartment. Grunge lunged toward me.

Mrs. T. grabbed my arm, dragging me inside. She tried to push the door closed. Grunge shoved his shoulder into the gap. I went to help Mrs. T., but

Grunge forced his way inside and slammed the door.

I backed down the hall. The music was so loud and wild that it seemed to be filling my head.

Grunge sneered and reached for me.

I turned and ran.

Mrs. T. barely got out of the way in time. I heard her screaming something at him in Russian. There was a *thump*.

I felt sick with fear and guilt because she'd gotten hurt trying to help me.

The living room was crowded with dark furniture and heaps of knickknacks. I sent a small table flying. China things smashed. I made for the window. One finger of winter sunlight promised freedom. If I could just get the window open and climb out . . .

Grunge grabbed me by my schoolbag and swung me around. My feet left the ground. I heard a thin scream. It was mine.

He shook me so hard I bit my tongue. Across the room, I could see Mrs. T. madly snapping the dolls apart, muttering to herself.

"Run!" I yelled at her.

Grunge laughed. It was a horrible sound. He shook me, pulling my sweater tight around my throat. I couldn't breathe. Music squealed — a crazy rush of wild violins. Everything roared in my ears. Spots spun in time to the music.

I'd never fainted before.

Next thing I knew, it was all quiet except for the sound of a clock ticking. Then I remembered Grunge and sat up, my heart in my throat.

I was on the floor, wedged between the couch and the glass-fronted cabinet full of little dolls like the one Mrs. T. had given me. Their pretty, painted faces smiled down at me.

Where was Grunge? Was Mrs. T. all right?

"You awake now, girlie." She smiled, beckoning me.

I stood up. We were alone.

"Where's Grunge? Did he hurt you?"

"He go. Matrioshka look after you."

Feeling sick, I stumbled around the couch and sat down. My shoes crunched on broken china. "I'm sorry, Mrs. T."

She smiled and pushed the doll into my hands.

I tried to give it back. "I'll be late for school."

"Matrioshka look after you." Mrs. T. put her hands on mine and popped the biggest doll apart. Crazy.

Her fingers urged me to open the next doll.

What if Grunge was waiting for me outside?

Pop. The second doll came apart.

He knew where I lived now.

Pop. The third doll opened.

I'd never escape him.

Mrs. T.'s fingers signaled me to open the fourth doll.

Pop.

I stared at the fifth doll. He had short, black hair and a sneering face.

"He all gone," Mrs. T. told me. "Matrioshka look after you."

I turned to stare at the cabinet behind me, crowded with little Russian dolls. Finally, I understood their secret.

About the Illustrators

The Story Illustrator
Steven Woolman

Steven Woolman designs and illustrates books for children. His many books include **The Watertower, Caleb,** and **One Child.** Steven is color-blind and his house is haunted. He loves the macabre and "twisted," and revels in science fiction and horror: "I enjoy anything that takes me where I never expected to go. If it surprises, shocks, or tingles my nerves, then I'm left begging for more."

The Cover Illustrator
Marc McBride

Marc McBride has illustrated covers for several magazines and children's books. Marc currently creates the realistic images for his covers using acrylic ink with an airbrush. To solve his messy studio problem, he plans to use computer graphics instead.